Funny Face Sunny Face

For Eskil, and not forgetting Bo
S.S.
For Rachel, with much love
R.B.

First published in 2015 by Nosy Crow Ltd

The Crow's Nest, 10a Lant Street

London SE1 1QR

www.nosycrow.com

ISBN 978 0 85763 254 8 (HB)

ISBN 978 0 85763 273 9 (PB)

Nosy Crow and associated logos are trademarks and/or registered trademarks

of Nosy Crow Ltd.

Text copyright © Sally Symes 2015

Illustrations copyright © Rosalind Beardshaw 2015

The right of Sally Symes to be identified as the author of this work

and of Rosalind Beardshaw to be identified as the illustrator of this work has been asserted.

A CIP catalogue record for this book is available

from the British Library.

Printed in China
Papers used by Nosy Crow are made from wood
grown in sustainable forests.

1 3 5 7 9 8 6 4 2 (HB)

1 3 5 7 9 8 6 4 2 (PB)

Funny Face Sunny Face

Sally Symes

Illustrated by

Rosalind
Beardshaw

nosy crow

Bunny face,

sunny face,

wake up . . .

. . . with a
funny face!

Bear
hair,

fair
hair,

hardly
any
there
hair.

Happy
ears,

flappy
ears,

funny,
wear-a-nappy ears.

New teeth,
chew teeth,

only one or
two teeth.

Hairy feet,

scary feet,

pitter-patter,
fairy feet.

Long legs,

strong legs . . .

. . . dancing-to-a-song legs!

Clinging hands,
swinging hands,

playing-ball-with-
flinging hands.

Sticky lips, licky lips,

love-you,
kiss-me-quicky lips.

Peeky nose,

beaky nose,

rub-a-
dub-a-
cheeky nose.

Nosy heads,

cosy heads,

all tired out . . .

. . . and
dozy
heads.